DAT

Five Funny Bunnies

Three Bouncing Tales

By **Jean Van Leeuwen**

Pictures by **Anne Wilsdorf**

Marshall Cavendish Children

For Juniper Rose — J.V.L.

For Louise and Olive — A.W.

Text copyright © 2012 by Jean Van Leeuwen
Illustrations copyright © 2012 by Anne Wilsdorf
All rights reserved
Marshall Cavendish Corporation
99 White Plains Road, Tarrytown, NY 10591
www.marshallcavendish.us/kids

The illustrations are rendered in watercolor and
china ink on white paper.

Book design by Vera Soki
Editor: Melanie Kroupa

Printed in Malaysia (T)
First edition
10 9 8 7 6 5 4 3 2 1

 Marshall Cavendish
Children

Library of Congress Cataloging-in-Publication Data
Van Leeuwen, Jean.
 Five funny bunnies : three bouncing tales / by Jean
Van Leeuwen ;
illustrated by Anne Wilsdorf. — 1st ed.
   p. cm.
 Summary: Relates three stories of young rabbit
siblings Flossie, Homer, Henry, Little George, and
Baby Sadie as they visit their grandmother, show off
their daring stunts, and play house.
 ISBN 978-0-7614-6114-2 (hardcover)
 ISBN 978-0-7614-6115-9 (ebook)
[1. Rabbits—Fiction. 2. Brothers and sisters—
Fiction.] I. Wilsdorf, Anne, ill. II. Title.
PZ7.V3273Fiv 2012   [E]—dc23   2011038376

Pie

Mrs. Rabbit had five little bunnies.

Oh my, they were HOPPY.

And FLOPPY. And DROPPY. And SLOPPY.

The littlest one was always GLOPPY.

One day Mrs. Rabbit said,
"Who wants to go to Grandma's house?"
"Me!" said Flossie.
"Me! Me!" said the twins, Homer and Henry.
"Me!" said Little George.
"Me, too!" said Baby Sadie.

So Mrs. Rabbit and the five little bunnies
baked Grandma a nice big berry pie.

Then she dressed them
in their best little suits and dresses
and piled them into the bunny baby buggy.
And off they went.

But it was a long way to Grandma's house.
The little bunnies got to feeling HOPPY.
Out they POPPED.

They played hopscotch and bunny tag
and who-can-hop-highest.
They hippity-HOPPED
till they flippity-FLOPPED in the grass.

"Children!" called Mrs. Rabbit.
Back into the bunny baby buggy they POPPED.

But Flossie was bossy. "Move over!" she said.
"You can't make us," said Homer and Henry.
The bunnies pinched and poked
and pulled each other's whiskers until . . .
all five bunnies fell out of the bunny baby buggy.

"Bad little bunnies!" scolded Mrs. Rabbit.
She piled them back into the bunny baby buggy.
"Don't anyone move a whisker," she said.
The five little bunnies sat oh so still . . .

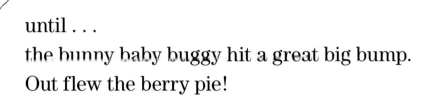

until . . .

the bunny baby buggy hit a great big bump.
Out flew the berry pie!

And then . . .

. . . it dropped, ker-PLOP!
right on TOP of the five little bunnies.

"Oh me, oh my!" said Mrs. Rabbit.
"Well, we might as well finish it off."
"Mmm," said Homer and Henry.
"That was yummy!"

"Who are these funny blue bunnies?" asked Grandma.

"It's us!" said the five little bunnies.

"But we lost the berry pie we baked for you."

"That's all right, my honey bunnies," said Grandma.

"Because I baked a cherry pie for YOU!"

So they all had cherry pie.
And everyone was happy
and HOPPY and FLOPPY
and DROPPY and SLOPPY.

And the littlest one got really, really GLOPPY.

Tricks

The five little bunnies went out to play.
"Look at me!" said Little George.
He zoomed up and down
and round and round
till he got so dizzy, he fell down.

"That was pretty good," said Flossie.
"But look at me!"
She jumped.
"One, two, three, WHEEE!"

"Not bad," said Homer and Henry.

"But look at us!"
They bounced like balls.
BOING! over the flowerpots.
BOING! over the berry bush.
BOING! all the way to the top of the wall.

Suddenly they heard, "BOO-HOO!"

"What's the matter?" said Flossie.

"Do you want carrot juice?" said Homer.

"A cookie?" said Henry.

"Your bunny baby?" said Little George.

Baby Sadie shook her head.

"Me, too!" she said.
"You, too?" said Homer and Henry.
"What can YOU do?"

Baby Sadie sat up straight.
She twitched her nose.
She wiggled her ears.
And . . .

she HOPPED.
"Her first hop!" said Flossie.
"Mama, come and see!"
Baby Sadie hopped again.
And again.
And again.

"Hooray!" cheered Mrs. Rabbit and the bunnies.
"That was the best trick of all," said Little George.

Nap Time

"I'll be the mother," said Flossie,
"and you can be the babies."

"Okay," said Homer and Henry.
"Can we play ball?"
"Trucks?" said Little George.
"Hop?" said Baby Sadie.

"STOP!" cried Flossie.
"I'm the mother, and I say
it's time for your nap."
She tucked them all into bed
and covered them with their
bunny baby blankets.
"Now go to sleep," she said.
"I'm going to make supper."

"Mama!" called Homer and Henry.
"What is it, babies?" said Flossie.
"We're too hot," said Homer and Henry.
"I'm too cold," said Little George.
So she fixed their blankets.

"Want juice!" said Baby Sadie.
"We're thirsty, too," said Homer and Henry.
So she brought them juice.

"My ear itches," said Little George.
"Want bunny baby!" said Baby Sadie.
"Oh dear," said Flossie.
"It's hard being a mother."

"I could tell you a story," she said.
"But you'll have to lie very still."
"We will," said the babies.

"Once there was a beautiful princess," said Flossie.
"And she lived in a great big castle."
"Who wants a princess?" said Homer and Henry.
"We want a dragon!"

"Of course there was a dragon," said Flossie.
"The meanest, scariest one you ever saw."
"Was it as big as a fire truck?" asked Little George.
"Bigger," said Flossie.
"Did it have sharp teeth?" asked Homer.
"A hundred sharp teeth," said Flossie.

"Did it have fire coming out of its mouth?" asked Henry.
"So hot it could burn down the castle," said Flossie.

"OOOOH!" said the babies.

"Was the princess scared?" asked Little George.

"Yes, she was," said Flossie.

"But she knew what to do about dragons."

"She gave it a blanket and a glass of juice
and told it a nice long story.
And guess what?"
"What?" the babies asked.

"The dragon got to feeling sleepy.
It got sleepier and sleepier,
and the fire in its mouth got smaller and smaller
until . . .
POOF! It went out.
Then the princess brushed her teeth and went to bed."

"AHHHH!" said the babies.
And then . . .
Homer's eyes closed.
Henry's eyes closed.
Little George's eyes closed.
"And she lived happily ever after," said Flossie.
And her eyes closed, too.

All the bunnies lay oh so still.
Except Baby Sadie, who said,

"The end."